The NAUGHTIEST ever Fairy

Written and illustrated by

Nick Ward

meadowside

York St John

CHILDREN'S BOOKS

igh on a green hill, in a little
yellow house, lived the naughtiest
ever fairy. After a busy morning
thinking up tricks and mixing
spells, the naughtiest ever
fairy liked to take a nap.

z z z Z Z Z Z z z z

Across the valley, in a big, blue
castle, lived the very noisy giant.
He spent the morning hard at work
with his very noisy chores but,
when his chores were done, the
very noisy giant loved to dance.

Every afternoon, just as the naughtiest ever fairy climbed into bed and closed her eyes, the very noisy giant would put on his favourite noisy music. Then he would skip and spin in his giant boots...

CRASH!

BANG!

It was getting harder and harder for the
naughtiest ever fairy to get any sleep at all.

CLUMP!

RATTLE!
CLATTER! CRASH!

The naughty fairy woke with a jump.
She had had enough. She couldn't get
her beauty sleep and it was starting
to show. As you can imagine, the
naughty fairy was getting very grumpy!

"If the giant wasn't so BIG," she thought,
"he wouldn't make so much NOISE!"
And that gave the fairy a naughty idea.

Soon it would be the giant's birthday, so the fairy sat down to make a special card and inside she wrote a very naughty spell...

naughty ♡ fairy

...in fact, the spell was so naughty that I can't tell you what it said until the magic has worn off!

"That should do the trick," smiled the naughty fairy, and she popped it in the post-box.

On his birthday, the noisy giant danced down the stairs. Just then a card popped through the letter-box.

"Yippee!" he cried (giants don't get many birthday cards, you see). "Who's it from?"

"Oh no!" said the giant. "I forgot. I can't read!" So the noisy giant went to find someone very clever who *could* read.

"Can you read my card?"
he asked the big, bad wolf.
"Of course," growled the wolf importantly,
as he grabbed the card from the giant's hand.
"I'm a very good reader!"

"What does it say?" asked the giant.
"Hold on, I've got to read it to myself first,"
growled the big, bad wolf.
And suddenly Kazam!
The big, bad wolf changed...

...into a timid little baa-lamb!

"How embarrassing!" shivered the gentle little lamb.

"I'm supposed to be fierce and ferocious!"

And he ran away to hide.

The noisy giant still didn't know

what his card said, so he went to see...

Baa!

...the bold and roaring lion
(who was king of the jungle).
"Can you read my card?" asked the very noisy giant.
"Of course," roared the lion imperiously.
"I'm a very good reader!"
He opened the card and started to read.
KaZam! The lion changed...

...into a little scaredy-cat!
"Oh, how humiliating!"
he meowed, running off
to hide. "I'm supposed to
be the king of the jungle!"
But still the noisy giant
didn't know what his
card said, so he
went to see...

...the last of the fiery dragons.

"Can you read my card?" asked the giant.

"Of course," said the dragon, grandly.

"I'm a very good reader!"

But as soon as he started
to read the message, Kazam!

The fiery dragon changed...

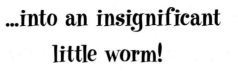

...into an insignificant little worm!

"Oh, this is insufferable!" squirmed the worm, crawling into his tiny hole. "I'm supposed to be a fiery dragon!" The poor giant still didn't know what his card said, so he went to see...

...the naughtiest ever fairy.

"Giant!" she gasped, very surprised to see him still so big and noisy. "Didn't you get your card?"

"Yes," said the giant. "But I can't read it. Can you help?"

"No chance," said the
fairy. "I'm not falling
for that old trick.
Find someone else
to read it for you..."

Kazam!

(oh you didn't, did you?)

For Colin and Denise

N.W.

First published in 2004 by
Meadowside Children's Books
185 Fleet Street, London, EC4A 2HS

Text and Illustrations © Nick Ward 2004

A CIP catalogue record for this book
is available from the British Library
Printed in China

10 9 8 7 6 5 4